YOUNG LIONS

written and illustrated by **Toshi Yoshida**

A woodblock print.

HOUGHTON MIFFLIN COMPANY BOSTON

Atlanta   Dallas   Geneva, Illinois   Palo Alto   Princeton   Toronto

Under a shady tree a pride of lions rests from the hot African sun. Some nap peacefully, while small cubs play at their sides. But three young lions are restless.

Their mother is napping, too. Tired of chasing games and hide and seek, they decide to set out on their first hunt alone.

On a nearby hill Father Lion sits on a sun-warmed rock. This is his territory.

Although he does not move, his eyes follow the young lions as they start across the grassy plain.

On their way they see a rhinoceros mother with her baby. Tick birds rest on her back. The lions do not go any closer. Rhinoceroses cannot see well, but their noses and ears are keen.

The wanderers come upon a herd of water buffaloes. At their feet are cattle egrets feeding unafraid of the larger animals. The buffaloes stare at the young lions as they quietly move through the grass.

7

In a wide field a group of zebras has gathered. The three young lions
hide themselves in the deep brush and try to get as close to the zebras
as they can.

But the alert zebras see the hiding lions, and the entire herd runs off through the trees.

Suddenly, a herd of impalas dashes across the plain. Something is chasing them!

In the antelope family impalas are among the fastest at running away.
The lions crouch and watch as the impalas run and leap past them.

Now two cheetahs come flying by at lightning speed, chasing the impalas. The lions could never run that fast.

Cheetahs are good hunters and good runners, but they cannot run for very long. This time the impalas will not be caught.

Out on the open plain, the lions come upon a flock of vultures eating
a dead zebra.

14

A lone hyena snarls at them. He wants the zebra, too, but there are too many vultures and he backs away.

Across the plain, the young lions see a large herd of animals. As they draw closer, they see that the animals have horns like cows and manes like horses. They are gnus.

Now big sister lion wanders away from the other two lions. She makes
a wide circle to the far side of a forest. The other lions crouch down
and little by little creep closer to the herd of gnus.

Suddenly a gnu dashes away. She has caught the scent of the young lions.

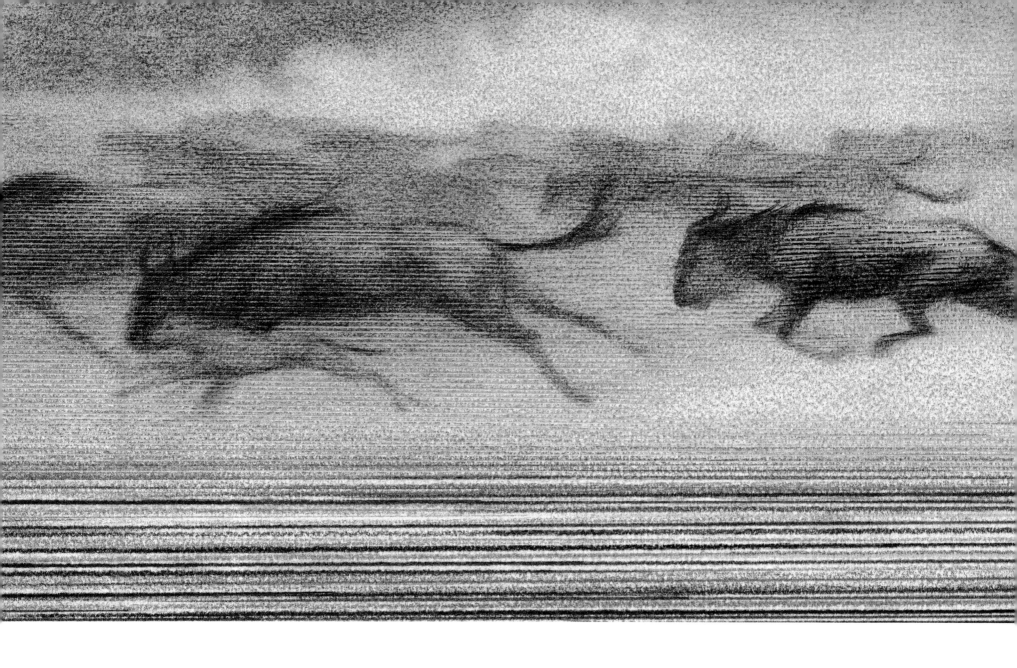

Then the entire herd rushes away from the forest toward the plains.
The baby gnus keep up, running as fast as their parents.

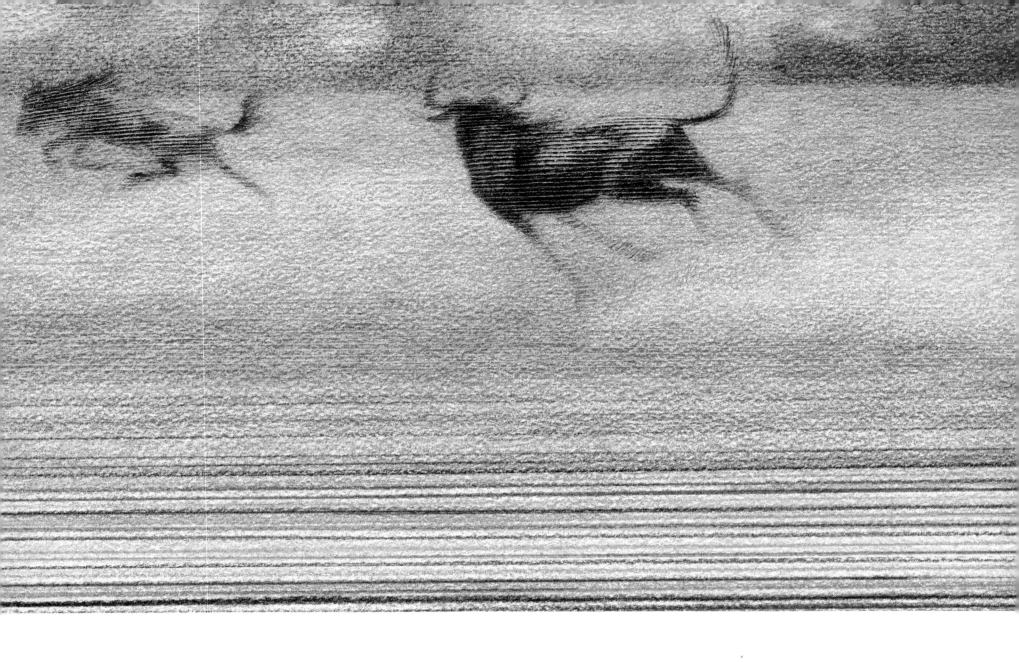

With their black manes flying, the gnus run away from the young lions.

Big sister lion runs after the gnus, but she cannot catch up with them.

The gnus disappear far away in a cloud of dust. The young lions now know how hard hunting is. Even for strong, grown-up lions more animals escape than are caught. The sound of the gnus' feet dies away. The grassy plain is silent again.

The lions wander on as evening comes. Now the sun settles behind
Mt. Kilimanjaro.

Herds of elephants and giraffes, antelopes and water buffaloes graze on
grass and trees.

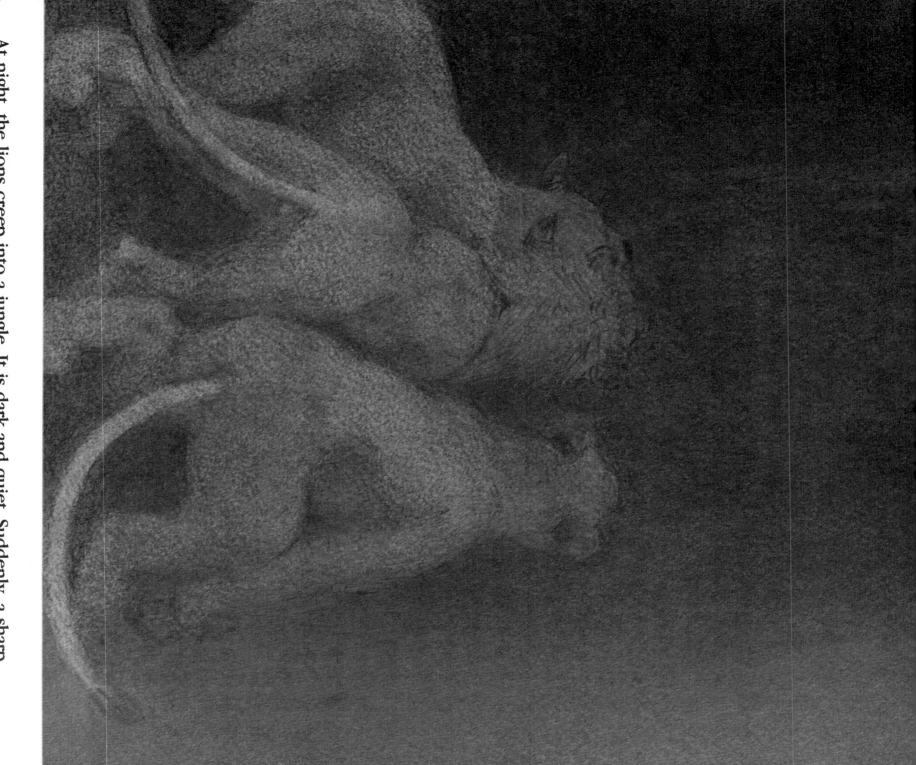

At night, the lions creep into a jungle. It is dark and quiet. Suddenly, a sharp screech echoes through the trees. High up in the branches of a dark tree, two eyes are staring at them. It is a leopard. He has caught an antelope.

26

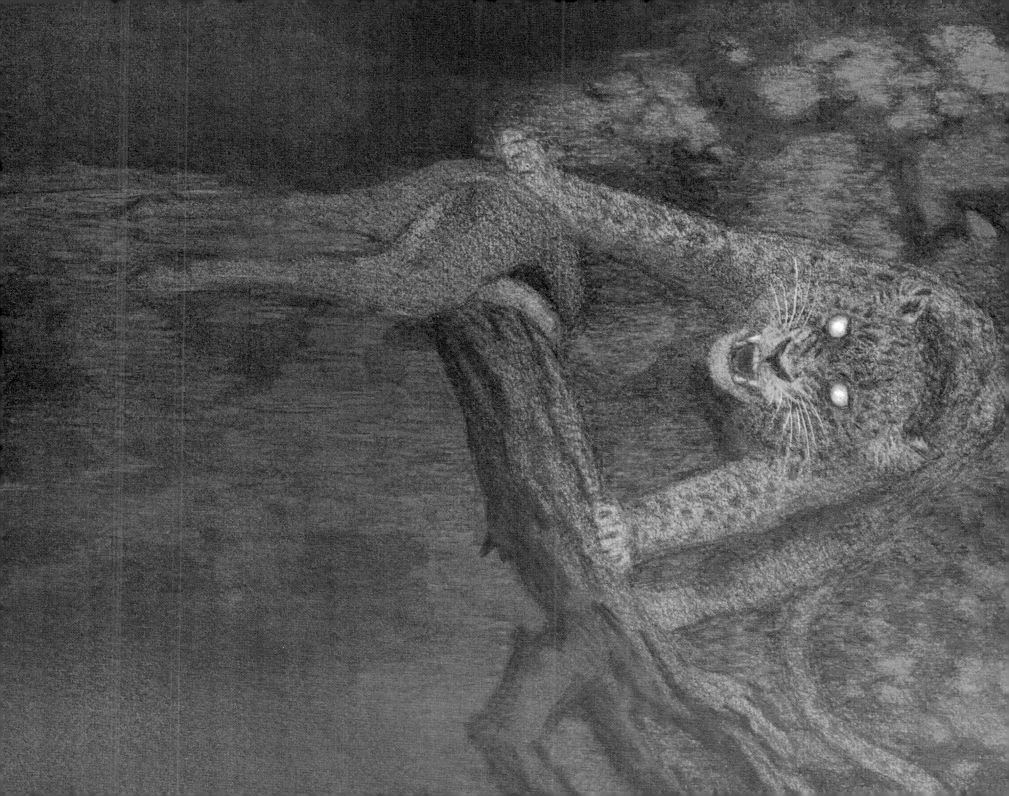

Startled by the leopard, the three young lions start home. On their way, they see a strange animal that curls up into a prickly ball as they surround it.

Little brother paws at the animal, but draws back as the porcupine's needles prick his paw. The lions leave the porcupine and continue home.

As they approach their own territory, they see Mother Lion waiting for them. The young lions run to her and lick her. They are glad to be home.

On their first hunt, they have seen many animals and have had many surprises.
Yet there is still much to learn that Father and Mother Lion will teach them.
Someday the three will be able to survive on their own on the grassy plains.

31

ISBN 0-395-61762-6

456789-B-96 95 94 93